THIS IS THE HOUSE THAT JACK BUILT

Paradise Found-beautiful post & beam Farmhse on approx. 51+ magnificent acs. Lovely level land w/lrg pond stocked with fish. This 4 BR, 2.5 bth, 2 fpl house is nestled amongst flowering trees, shrubs & perennials. Anderson French wood SGD's open to decks in almost every room-truly unique. What views! What wildlife abounds! Seen by appt only. Please call listing agt Elisa Sumner 277...

SIMPLY ELEGANT
Beautifully sited on prime 19 acres in the heart of Bedford. Glamorous shingle style 6000+ sf of quality construction. Oversized living room w/fpl. Enormous gourmet's kitchen. Lavish master suite w/sitting room, fpl &

Master bath. $2.995M (2105136)
STUNNING CONTEMPORARY
Architect designed & set on over 3 acs of prof'lly landscpd seclusion in Lewisboro. Magnificent dropped LR w/20' ceil, formal DR, sunlit kit adj solarium b'fast room which leads to outside liv spaces & spa. 3 fpls, 2-story office/studio w/sep entrance. Winter views of ... $1.2M (2108562)

ENTIRE 4 STORY TOWNHSE
W/PRIVATE 1,000 SQ FT GARDEN
Steps to Central Pk, 5th & Madison Ave shopping. Turn of the century house w/ 4BR's, 4 full baths & 2 powder rooms. Sep maid's quarters or perfect home office. Family...

18th Century Manor House
Historically-significant, meticulously-restored 15-rm brick Georgian on 6+ acres. Prof'l kitch, elegant bths, new mechanicals. 19th C caretaker's wing. Ask $1,100,000
M. Woods bkr 212-445-...

...re by legendary H. T. Lindeberg.
Architect Designed
On a quiet lane, this spectacular home faces south and draws wonderful light overlooking 4 beautiful acres. 2-story cathedral ceiling center hall; fireplaces

EXTRAORDINARY FARM.
Early salt-box-style house w/scrnd porch, deck, many improves. 124 rolling acres with fenced horse pastures, hayfields, woods. Small barn w/apt above, huge horse barn ...

Palenville Gorgeous Escape. Hdwd flrs, fpl, 3BR, full bsmt, fab sett'g, mins to Woodstock, state preserve & skl'g. $97.5K Greene County Rlty

www.gracepost.com
C. 1800 CENTER HALL COLONIAL
5000 sf brick. Wide CH with Palladian window. Exquisite detail: 15 rms, 5 fplcs, 5 baths. Guest house with fplc. 2 artist's studios. 3-car gar. Barn. Shop. Multi-lines & LAN for home profession. Ancient trees and organic gardens everywhere. Long tree-lined drive. Wonderful country estate. .... $1.185M.
COLDWELL BANKER

UNDERSTATED ELEGANCE
Located on open Long Island sound and sited on a gentle rise this gracious custom bit in 1956, and sits majestically on 1.3 acres of premier waterfront property. The unobstructed views encompass Larchmont Harbor, umbrella point & the sound. The well maintained interior boasts a large living rm with fireplace and bay window flanked by doors to the patio, a ...

A COUNTRY JEWEL
Fabulous country contemporary with exquisite gardens & decks galore. 3 BRs, 3 baths & fplc. Totally secluded on 6 acres. Priced to sell quickly. $295,000.
CHATHAM PROPERTIES

BREATHTAKING "Napa Valley-esque" views in a secluded, tranquil setting. Glass & log w/soaring ceilings & massive stone fplc. 40x40 studio/out-building. 9+ acres of paradise. $450,000.
FLEMMING REALTY

COUNTRY QUIET
One look at this sprawling 6BR, 3.5Bth Contemp. framed by mature trees & specimen plantings on 1.40acs in desired estate area & you'll be hooked on country life. Custom bit for lavish entertain/comfortable family living, this 15yr "young" residence boasts vaulted ...

ATTRACTIVE PRICE
Redecorated decor, refinished flrs & new KIT appliances. Set on almost .5 acre in a most convenient location. 4BDs, 3.5bths, LR w/fpl, DR, KIT w/ breakfast area opens to deck, Master w/whirlpool bth, lower level Rec room w/wet bar, ...

Joyce 56mm eves 203 ...
EXTRA SPECIAL
41 Winthrop Dr...One of Riverside's most desirable streets, renov. Colonial, state-of-art kitchen & fam. rm, 4BRs, 2.5bths, a/c. CB#GFP5075 .... $1,625,000
Eileen O'Connor eves 203...

SUNDAY 1-3PM
Lovely old & charming Colonial in the Huntswood area, feat 4BR's, 2 baths EIK, LR/fpl, hdwd flrs, wond htd prch new heating systm, 2-car gar & privacy Near train, bus & shops. $349,500 dir:Cross County Prkwy to Gramatan ...#11 Ridgeway Street

GENTLY RUSHING STREAM to beautiful country pond. Age-old trees, rock outcroppings & old stone walls. The quintessential country setting! 4 picturebook acs. Beautifully renovated country hse with slate hrdwd flrs & wonderful open flr plan by award-winning builder. Dramatic Great Rm with Fpl & Dining Area with magnificent light, Octagonal Sun Rm, Cntry Kit, 1st flr MBR Ste, Guest Ste with Fpl. Office, 2 add'l BR, Gar with Studio . . . $1,450,000

AWARD-WINNING HOME...impeccable design, superior materials & the finest workmanship. State-of-art kit. 5BRs. 6F/2Hbths, MBR Suite w/fpl & prvt deck. Indr & outdr pools. 2.25 flat acres w/stone walls & prof lndscping. See Virtual Tour @coldwellbanker.com CB#NCN0443 . . . . $2,395,000
COLDWELL BANKER

RENOVATED FARMHOUSE
Bright, light, spacious. 4 or 5 BRs, 3 full BAs, lrg eat-in country Kit. Great yard with bulbs, perennials, flowering shrubs & trees, babbling brook. Worth the ride. $199,000.

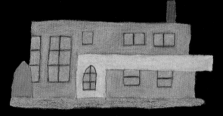

MAGNIFICENT CONTEMPORARY
Private 5 BR, 3 bath has 20' ceilings, great room w/walls of glass, fplcs, guest apt. Pool, tennis, great mtn vus. Convenient Capital area. . . . . $695,000.
THE ANDERSON AGENCY

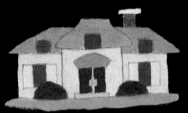

FRENCH MANOR HOME
Architecturally distinctive w/European feeling. Stone residence superbly set around a pretty courtyard enjoys privacy of 4+ ac in prestigious Waccabuc

Stone Ridge. Charming country house secluded on 20 acres. Built 1920's w/new addition in brick. 8 BRs, 6 baths, 6 fplcs. on 6.7 ac. Elegant, spacious 1600s stone house w/kingsboard flrs, FPs in LR & DR. Sep cottage o'looks inground pool & hot tub. Pond + stream nr paddock. Reduced: $449,000.

PACKED WITH POTENTIAL
Comfortable and quality are just two of the many words that will come to mind when you see this ranch style residence. Set on a deep lot, this 2 bedroom, 2 bath house has a large living room, a heated solarium, an inviting eat-in kitchen and central air

Gracious New Rocking Chair front Porch Farmhouse Colonial set on 3.25 acs. Double height foyer w/beautiful curved staircase, LR/Mrble Fpl, DR Fam Rm/Fpl, Custom EIK w/Butler's

ty. $1900/mo. 212-925-4340, 845-756-8229
PEACEFUL COUNTRY RETREAT
PLEASANT VALLEY. On Scenic Horse Prop. c. 1840, 4 BR, 3000 SF Farmhse. Overlook ponds, fields—just off TSP. $2000/mo + utils.
Columbia County

www.columbiacountryhomes.com
ROMANTIC HIDEAWAY
Charming 3BR 1950's cottage. LR with FP, hdwd flrs. Spectacular 10 ac setting, huge pond, glorious gardens, wildflower meadow. Totally private, totally wonderful. $299,000.
http://www.oldabent.com

Impeccable Cape w/sep in-law suite, very flex flr plan, LR/fpl, DR/blt-ins, new kit, FR w/slider to deck. 3 BRs + den, 3.1bths. In law suite, kit, LR w/fpl stairs to MBR w/fpl & Jacuzzi. Low taxes on cul-de-sac. Close to town.
NEW LISTING $599,000
Young 4BR, 2.5bth Col on luscious lvl prop. Updated & tastefully decorated. The cntry kit w/fplc

SIMPLY ELEGANT
Beautifully sited on prime 19 acres in the heart of Bedford. Glamorous shingle style 6000+ sf of quality

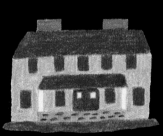

Chrmg gracious Pre-Rev. Farmhse, blt 1750, top estate area, 3.20ac, quiet cntry rd, 5 min to RR & shops; artist studio cottage. DIR: I-684N, X4, L on Rte 172, L on Saries St, R on Byram Lake Rd, 1st hse on L. #266. CB#BEF1911 . . . $909,000

STEP INTO THE PAST! Circa 1860 Farmhouse. Beautifully proportioned rms & period details. Hrdwd flrs, 2 Fpls, wonderful ceiling height. Formal DR with fabulous millwork. LR & FamRm with Fpls. Gourmet Kit with Butler's Pantry. Exceptional MBR Suite with custom built-ins & Bth. 4BRs. Central air. John Jay Schools. Walk to the reservation. Just listed. . . . $549,000

www.richoreirealestate.com
WOODSTOCK area. Secluded contemp on 6+ acres w/glorious views. Cathedral LR/fplc. 2 BRs, 2 baths. Screened porch, deck, inground pool. $350,000.
Call Gale @ Eichborn Rlty 845-679-8800

MAGNIFICENT TOWNHOUSE
Grand lifestyle steps to the park! Eleg 4sty brnstn, parlor/gdn duplx. Custom kit,fine mahogany,grand LR,deck & gdn + 2 hi inc rntls. Xlnt cond $1,425,000

STARRING IN NO PARTICULAR ORDER...

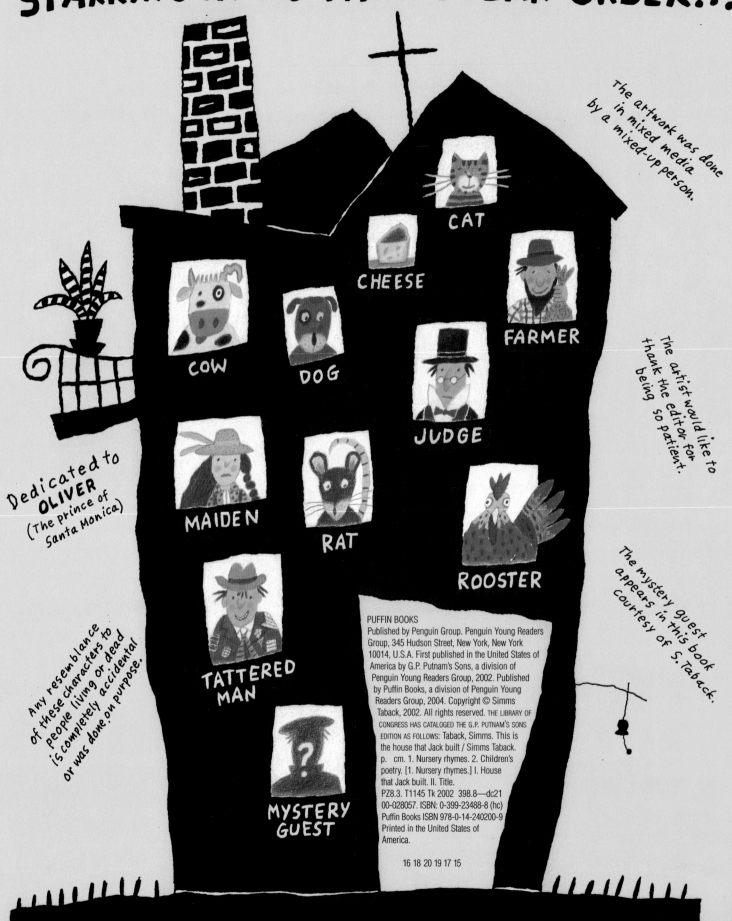

CAT

CHEESE

FARMER

COW

DOG

JUDGE

MAIDEN

RAT

ROOSTER

TATTERED MAN

MYSTERY GUEST

The artwork was done in mixed media by a mixed-up person.

The artist would like to thank the editor for being so patient.

The mystery guest appears in this book courtesy of S. Taback.

Dedicated to **OLIVER** (The prince of Santa Monica)

Any resemblance of these characters to people living or dead is completely accidental or was done on purpose.

PUFFIN BOOKS
Published by Penguin Group. Penguin Young Readers Group, 345 Hudson Street, New York, New York 10014, U.S.A. First published in the United States of America by G.P. Putnam's Sons, a division of Penguin Young Readers Group, 2002. Published by Puffin Books, a division of Penguin Young Readers Group, 2004. Copyright © Simms Taback, 2002. All rights reserved. THE LIBRARY OF CONGRESS HAS CATALOGED THE G.P. PUTNAM'S SONS EDITION AS FOLLOWS: Taback, Simms. This is the house that Jack built / Simms Taback. p. cm. 1. Nursery rhymes. 2. Children's poetry. [1. Nursery rhymes.] I. House that Jack built. II. Title. PZ8.3. T1145 Tk 2002 398.8—dc21 00-028057. ISBN: 0-399-23488-8 (hc) Puffin Books ISBN 978-0-14-240200-9 Printed in the United States of America.

16 18 20 19 17 15

THIS IS THE HOUSE THAT JACK BUILT

SIMMS TABACK

PUFFIN BOOKS

THIS IS THE HOUSE THAT JACK BUILT.

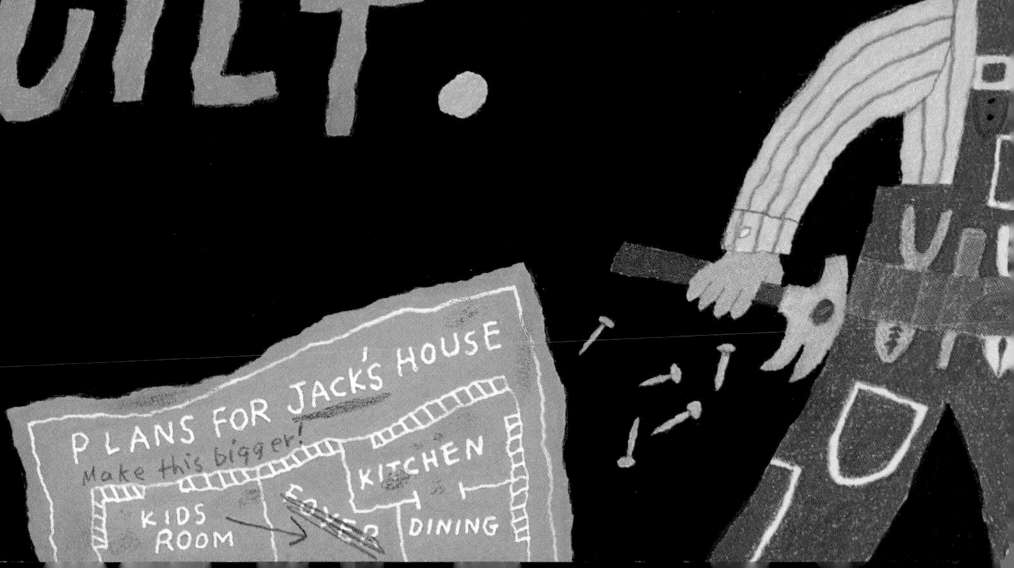

THIS IS THE CHEESE

smelly

Not so smelly

A little smelly

CHEDDAR

GOUDA

SWISS

Stinky

yummy

Sort of yechhy

CAMEMBERT

AMERICAN CHEESE

MUENSTER

Really stinky

Just smelly

Smelly and stinky

← and gooey

BRIE

FONTINA

PORT-SALUT

THAT LAY
IN THE
HOUSE THAT
JACK BUILT.

Call Jack for key

THAT ATE
THE CHEESE
THAT
LAY IN
THE HOUSE
THAT
JACK BUILT.

PHEW

Call
Jack
for key

THIS IS THE CAT

FELIX
One of the most famous comix characters.

MANX
A cat without a tail.

SIAMESE CAT
It needs lots of attention and love.

BOMBAY CAT
A very interesting pet with a jet-black coat.

BURMESE CAT
A cat for lovers of little cats.

CHESHIRE CAT
A very mysterious cat.

ALLEY CAT
A mixed breed and very independent.

SPHINX CAT
A hairless cat that looks like a pug dog.

MAINE COON
A very appealing and popular cat.

CAT IN HAT CAT
Goofy behavior- talks in rhyme.

HALLOWEEN CAT
A party cat for trick or treat.

KORAT CAT
A cat that brings good luck.

THAT KILLED
THE RAT
THAT
ATE
THE
CHEESE
THAT
LAY
IN THE HOUSE
THAT JACK BUILT.
Cheddar
1 99 lb.
Call Jack for key

THAT WORRIED
THE
CAT THAT
KILLED THE
RAT
THAT ATE THE
CHEESE
THAT LAY
IN THE HOUSE
THAT JACK
BUILT.

THAT TOSSED THE DOG
THAT WORRIED
THE CAT
THAT
KILLED THE RAT
THAT
ATE THE CHEESE
THAT LAY
IN THE HOUSE
THAT JACK BUILT.
MEE OW
MEOW

THIS IS THE MAIDEN ALL FORLORN

The Maiden

From the day
that she was born,
Whether night
or early morn,
She couldn't help
but be forlorn.

AND THIS IS THE ARTIST
A PICTURE OF THE
THAT KEPT THE ROOSTER THAT CROWED IN THE MORN
THAT MARRIED THE MAN ALL TATTERED AND TORN
THAT MILKED THE COW WITH THE CRUMPLED HORN
Guess who?
INDIA INK
CLEAN WATER
WHITE INDIA INK
GLUE
KNEADED ERASURE
SHAKER'S GARDEN SEED
SHAKER SEED CO
HINT: His name rhymes with "forget-me-not"!

THAT LAY
IN THE HOUSE
THAT JACK
BUILT.

THIS IS THE HOUSE THAT JACK BUILT, a favorite rhyme for children
for several centuries, was first published in 1755 and probably derived
from an ancient Hebrew chant in the 16th century.
It was illustrated by Randolph Caldecott in 1878.